The Buddy Bench

Henry   Lily   Mei   Pablo   Padma

by Gwendolyn Hooks

illustrated by Shirley Ng-Benitez

Lee & Low Books Inc.   New York

Dedicated to those with friends and those in need of a friend.
Reach out and have fun together. —G.H.

To the reader: find an undiscovered buddy in your class
or at recess and greet 'em with a smile. —S.N-B.

Text copyright © 2019 by Lee & Low Books Inc.
Illustrations copyright © 2019 by Shirley Ng-Benitez
All rights reserved. No part of this book may be reproduced, transmitted, or stored
in an information retrieval system in any form or by any means, electronic, mechanical,
photocopying, recording, or otherwise, without written permission from the publisher.
LEE & LOW BOOKS Inc., 95 Madison Avenue, New York, NY 10016, leeandlow.com
Book design by Maria Mercado
Book production by The Kids at Our House
The illustrations are rendered in watercolor and altered digitally
Manufactured in China by Imago
Printed on paper from responsible sources
(hc) 10 9 8 7 6 5 4 3 2 1
(pb) 10 9 8 7 6 5 4 3 2 1
First Edition

Library of Congress Cataloging-in-Publication Data
Names: Hooks, Gwendolyn, author. | Ng-Benitez, Shirley, illustrator.
Title: The buddy bench / by Gwendolyn Hooks; illustrated by Shirley Ng-Benitez.
Description: First edition. | New York: Lee & Low Books Inc., [2019] |
  Series: [Dive into reading ; 7] | Summary: When Padma notices a boy
  sitting by himself every day, she enlists her friends to create a buddy
  bench, where anyone at school can go if they want or need a friend.
Identifiers: LCCN 2018049338 | ISBN 9781620145715 (Hardcover)
  ISBN 9781620145722 (Paperback)
Subjects: | CYAC: Benches—Fiction. | Schools—Fiction. | Friendship—Fiction.
Classification: LCC PZ7.H76635 Bud 2019 | DDC [E]—dc23
LC record available at https://lccn.loc.gov/2018049338

Contents

Old Friends

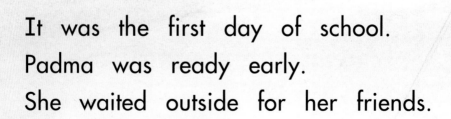

It was the first day of school.
Padma was ready early.
She waited outside for her friends.

"Have you been out here all night?"
asked Henry.

"No," said Padma.

"But I can't wait for school to start."

"Here come Mei, Lily, and Pablo,"
said Henry.

"Finally!" said Padma.
"Let's go!"

At school they looked
for their classroom.
"Oh no!" said Lily.
"We are all in the same class.
But not Padma."

"I'm next door," said Padma.
"You will be all alone," said Lily.
"It's okay," said Padma.
"I like to make new friends."

At lunch Padma sat with
her old friends.
"I see some of the kids
in my class," said Padma.

She waved them over to the table.
"I'm Pablo," said Pablo.
"Hi," said Padma's new friends.

At recess everyone played games.
Padma played with her old friends.
Padma played with her new friends.

They all jumped rope together.
It was a great first day of school.

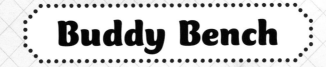

One day Padma saw a new boy
standing alone by the fence.
"I wonder why he's all alone,"
she said to Lily.

"It's not easy for everyone
to make new friends," said Lily.
The boy left before they could
say hi.

"I have an idea,"
said Padma.
"Let's make a place
where kids can go
if they feel lonely."

"What kind of place?" asked Mei.
"We can make a Buddy Bench!"
said Padma.

"Let's paint the bench," said Henry.
"Let's paint it yellow and purple,"
said Lily.
"Let's make a sign. Then everyone
will know where to go to meet
new friends," said Padma.

"We need to ask Principal Hart," said Pablo.
They went to the principal's office.
Principal Hart said the Buddy Bench was a great idea.

On Saturday, they painted the bench.
They made a Buddy Bench sign.

Then Padma made up a song
about the bench.

They sang the words as they
jumped rope.

After a few days everyone
was singing the song.
But no one sat
on the Buddy Bench.

New Friends

Weeks passed and still no one
sat on the Buddy Bench.
Then one day Padma
saw the new boy sitting
on the Buddy Bench.

"Let's go!" said Padma
to her friends.

"Hi! I'm Padma," said Padma.
"What's your name?"
"Zander," said the boy.

"Hi," said Mei. "Did you just move here?"

"Yes. My mom is an army
pilot," said Zander.
"We move around a lot."

"Moving is not always fun,"
said Lily.
"It's hard to make new friends."

"We would like to be
your friends," said Padma.
"Do you want to play?"
asked Zander.
"I like slides."
"Me too!" said Padma.

Padma played with her old friends.
Padma played with her new friends.
They all played together.

Activity

Have more fun with this book!

1. Was there a time when you helped someone who was lonely? Have you ever felt lonely? What did you do?

2. Does your school or a nearby park have a Buddy Bench? Do you think the Buddy Bench is a good idea? Why or why not?

3. With help from an adult, write a letter to the principal of your school about how a Buddy Bench could help students.

4. Think of another idea besides a Buddy Bench to help a new student make friends.